DANNY-DON'T JUMP!

DANNY- DON'T JUMP!

Hazel Townson

Illustrated by Amelia Rosato

Andersen Press • London

For Jack, Lucille and John Littlewood of St. Helier

Text © 1985 by Hazel Townson
Illustrations © 1985 by Amelia Rosato

First published in Great Britain in 1985 by
Andersen Press Limited,
20 Vauxhall Bridge Road, London SWIV 2SA
www.andersenpress.co.uk

This edition first published in 2005

British Library Cataloguing in Publication Data available
ISBN 1 84270 445 1

Printed and bound in Great Britain by Bookmarque Ltd.,
Croydon, Surrey

Contents

I
Creation

First there was the business of the cloakroom wash-bowl. All Danny did was to drop a football boot into it, quite accidentally. He never meant to cause a hundred pounds' worth of damage, and privately thought the washbowl must have been faulty to start with. Then there was the newly-planted sapling he walked into when he was seeing what it was like to be blind, and the pile of dirty plates that slid from his monitoring hands halfway through the second sitting of school dinner. (Well, *that* could have happened to anyone, and if folks would go leaving slippery lumps of gristle skidding about in gravy-puddles on every plate, then what could they expect?) But the fact was that by the time Danny broke the headmaster's window—and the Grecian vase that sat on the window-sill—he had already acquired a reputation, deserved or not, as a reckless vandal.

'I fail to understand,' said the headmaster, Mr Cropper, 'how you came to be hurling a Bible across the playground in the first place.'

Danny thought a man in Mr Cropper's position had

no business to fail to understand, especially when Danny himself had just explained that he had been late for assembly, where he was due to read out a psalm, and had slipped on the core of Reg Hopkinson's apple, which wasn't supposed to have been eaten until lunchtime anyway.

Mr Cropper frowned at Danny over his half-spectacles.

'Well, Danny, I must say I'm disappointed in you. I thought you had the makings of a first-rate sensible lad, but just lately you seem to have run completely off the rails. I think it's high time you turned over not so much a new leaf as a whole new plantation. In this school we're aiming for creation, not destruction. Bear that in mind. See if you can't manage to make some positive contribution . . . .'

Mr Cropper rambled on, but Danny had ceased to listen. The word 'creation' had caught on a hook in his mind, and his whole attention was bent on trying to shake it free.

Danny Lyndon really wanted to be liked, and to live up to other people's expectations. To this end he had suffered many things, such as doggedly learning to swim when he hated the water, sharing his crisps when he was ravenous and putting his precious limbs in the paths of lethal cricket balls. All of a sudden, it seemed, he had become unpopular by accident, and he found

that he wanted to set this right. Creation, eh? Some positive contribution? Well, at least he could start by repairing the Grecian vase with his new tube of Superglue. He would ask for the pieces at once.

'Sir! If you'll let me—!'

'No more excuses, Danny, please. Your ingenuity has already been stretched to the limit.'

'But if you'll just give me . . . .'

'Least said, soonest mended!' Mr Cropper clapped a monstrously heavy hand on to Danny's shoulder. 'Just remember, boy—actions speak louder than words.'

Well, thought Danny, that was true enough; that last slap of the Cropper's had shouted and screamed all the way through Danny's nervous system. The bell's deafening clang now added to the agony and Danny had to go, casting wistful backward glances at the Cropper's wastepaper basket, wherein reposed the shattered ornament.

Never mind; today was Friday. The Cropper went home promptly on Fridays because of his local history meeting, so Danny would sneak back after school and help himself to the broken bits of vase. What a lovely surprise for the Cropper when he got it back good as new on Monday morning!

At four o'clock Danny sneaked back all right, but he had reckoned without Mrs Bodge, who was busy cleaning the headmaster's office.

'What you doin' 'ere, then?' Mrs Bodge instantly smelled a rat. 'Come for a canin', have you? Well, he's gone, so happen it's your lucky day.'

Danny shook his head. 'They're not allowed to cane us any more. They have to forgive us, which is worse. They go on and on and *on*.' Danny proceeded to explain his errand.

'Broke his window and vase with a Bible, eh? Take a real Christian to forgive that!' Mrs Bodge began to chuckle, remembering that Mr Cropper went to yoga classes; he was probably a heathen.

'I *would* like to have a go at mending it.'

Danny edged towards the basket, looking so wistfully woebegone that Mrs Bodge took pity on him. Riffling through the basket, she picked out the vase bits and set them down on the Cropper's desk.

'There you are, then, and I wish you joy of it. Proper jig-saw puzzle that's going to be. Still, I saw one in a museum once, made up from a hundred and eighty pieces, and you'd never have known except it looked as though it was wearing a hairnet.'

'Thanks, Mrs Bodge!' Danny had dropped the pieces—(luckily there were only seven)—into a cast-off envelope from the same basket, and was heading for the door.

'And don't make an 'abit of it!' Mrs Bodge called after him.

At home, Danny spread out his seven pottery pieces on a sheet of newspaper on the kitchen table and carefully unscrewed the top of his Superglue. He began to stir the pieces around into some sort of shape.

'Oooh, that looks interesting! What is it?' asked Mrs Lyndon, who liked to think of herself as a caring mother.

'It's—er—a project. For art.'

'Well, I never! The things they think of at that school! There was none of that in our day, I can tell you! Proper boring old lessons we had. No chance to develop our artistic talents. You don't know how lucky you are!'

'Yes, I do. But don't stand watching, Mum. You'll make me nervous.'

'Go on with you! You're not nervous of *me*!' cried Mrs Lyndon playfully. 'I wouldn't care if I was always nagging you about dropping glue on the table and sticking your fingers together. I *trust* you. Anyway, you haven't told me what it is yet.'

'It's a Grecian vase.'

'Fancy! A sort of kit, is it? Like those pictures they paint by numbers? Well, you make a good job of it, son—(as I'm sure you will)—and you can put it on the mantelpiece in the front room.'

'I can't keep it, Mum. It's for school.'

'Well, surely they'll let you buy it when you've put all that work into it. They used to do that with our sewing and your dad's woodwork. I'll drop a line to Mr Cropper if you like, and ask him.'

'No, Mum!'

Fortunately, Danny's dad came home just then, and Mrs Lyndon bustled off to see to the dinner. Danny heaved a sigh of relief—but it didn't last long. He suddenly discovered that one piece of the vase—a vital bottom bit—was missing. What a rotten shame, just as he'd started to make the whole thing look quite presentable again! You'd think fate would help out a bit when you were trying to make amends. Well, that left Danny two alternatives. He could throw the whole thing into the dustbin and continue his life of shameful notoriety. Or he could go back to school and hunt for the missing piece. Maybe Mrs Bodge would still be there.

Sneaking off quietly, Danny ran all the way back to school, but he did remember to put the top back on his Superglue first.

2

Destruction

Alas! Mrs Bodge and her cronies had gone; that was the first thing Danny discovered. The whole place was locked up and there wasn't a soul about. The second thing he discovered was that the broken pane in the Cropper's window hadn't yet been replaced. The gap was covered with a sheet of thin plywood, which should not be too difficult to remove. In fact, it proved amazingly easy, as though someone had already had a go at it. A few minutes later Danny, feeling like the worst kind of criminal, yet mystifyingly pleased with himself all the same, was standing in the middle of the Cropper's office, having sellotaped the plywood back into place lest some passing nosey-parker should spot the gap.

So far, so good. Now all he had to do was to find the missing bit of vase. He dropped down on to his hands and knees and started a tour of the carpet, peering under desk and chairs, along bottom shelves and round the backs of cupboards. He did not find what he was looking for. Instead, he caught his foot in the telephone flex and dragged the telephone from the desk to the floor with a resounding clang. Immediately a flock of papers rose from the desk like great, white seabirds disturbed from their private cliff. Ominously they swerved and soared and settled all around the room. Danny crouched motionless, shielding his face in horror. Could they have been exam papers, placed in order of merit? Then, suddenly frantic with panic, Danny leapt to his feet and started chasing the bits of paper. One sheet tore as he tried to snatch it from under his foot, and another sheet managed to slip down behind the radiator where no human hand could follow.

It was whilst he was poking about behind the radiator with the Cropper's long, steel paper-knife that he stabbed clean through the lump of 'Plumber's Mate' gunge with which the caretaker had successfully stopped a recent leak. Water began to drip on to the carpet, then to run out at a faster rate, until a sizeable puddle collected.

How cruel Fate could be! From one small good intention the situation had grown into a hideous nightmare wherein Danny, in true nightmare fashion, found his thinking and his action paralysed. He did not know how long he sat there, gazing at the spreading patch of wet which began to lick the edges of more papers. But at last he roused himself and flew off to the kitchen for a mop.

Gone was the moment when Danny might have retreated and given up the struggle to make amends. Now he was so heavily involved in catastrophe that he simply had to put things right. But where was the mop? He had seen a dinner-lady using it that very day, to stem a river of watery custard flowing down the dining-room's centre aisle. But what had she done with that mop afterwards? Danny flung open all the cupboard doors in sight. He even looked in the fridge, reminding himself painfully of his missed meal. At last he remembered the broom-cupboard next to the kitchen door. He opened the broom-cupboard—and a body fell out.

'I can't think what's happened to our Danny,' said Mrs Lyndon, dishing up mounds of mashed potato. 'I never heard him go out, did you?'

'He'll be here as soon as he smells that dinner,' replied Mr Lyndon confidently. 'Never known him miss a meal.'

'If he's gone further than the gate he won't be *able* to smell it.'

'Well, stick his plate back in the oven. I don't see why we should wait. He knows the meal-times and he has a perfectly good watch.'

'It will all dry up in the oven.'

'Teach him the value of punctuality, then, won't it?'

Mrs Lyndon sighed. 'Here, you start your dinner,

then. I'll just give him a shout.'

She went to the front door and called her son's name. There being no reply, she walked down the path to the gate, then called again.

Esmée Bates, who was swinging on next door's gate, said: 'Your Danny's gone back to school.'

'At this time? Whatever for?'

Esmée shrugged and continued swinging.

'He went up School Lane. Nothing else up there that I know of.' Esmée was not quite as unobservant as she looked, though twice as cheeky.

'Well, if you see him, tell him his dinner's ready.'

Mrs Lyndon was not alarmed. She was even trying hard not to be annoyed. Perhaps Danny had forgotten something? A bit of his project, maybe? If he had gone back to school, no possible harm could come to him there. In fact, it was quite heartening, really, to think the lad was so keen on the place.

Having left school early that Friday, Mr Cropper drove first to the barber's, then home for his evening meal. After watching the teatime news on television, he showered and changed, then started packing his brief-case with the papers he needed for the local history meeting. It was his turn to speak tonight, and he had prepared a talk about Keevan Tower, a crumbling local monument about whose origin there was a deal of controversy. The name 'Keevan' was supposed to be a corruption of the French 'Qui vient?' (Who's coming?) but it was Mr Cropper's belief that this Tower had been built, not by the Normans as a Watch Tower, but in 1720 by a gentleman called Sir Cuthbert Keevayne, as a pseudo-Norman folly. Tonight, Mr Cropper intended to spring this information as a surprise upon his colleagues. For evidence, he had made a pile of copies of an ancient plan of the Tower with a quotation underneath it, referring to 'ye incredyble follye of Sir Cuthbt. Keevayne'. He had come across this evidence in an ancient volume dredged up from the back room of the local library, and since the librarian had told him nobody had even looked at the book for eighty years, he felt sure that his information would drop like a bomb-shell. In fact, the Cropper was hoping to make a bit of a name for himself as a local history researcher.

He stretched out a hand across the dressing-table to gather up this vital pile of copies—and encountered an empty space. He had left the dratted things at school!

'Serves you right for using the school photocopier for your private business,' sniffed his wife.

Mr Cropper looked at his watch. 'Never mind; I'll nip in and get them. Where are my school keys?' He calculated that there was half an hour before his meeting was due to start. Just enough time for the run to school, plus all the fiddle of unlocking and re-locking

the building. No time to waste, however. Mr Cropper
jumped into his car, having aimed a brief farewell peck
at his wife's cheek, and set off at once.

He had not gone more than a couple of hundred
metres when he was flagged down by the vicar, who
had just set out on foot for the local history meeting.
(The vicar himself could not afford to run a car, but
had been secretary of the Local History Society for
more years than anyone could remember.)

There was no help for it; Mr Cropper would have to
offer the vicar a lift. He pulled up, forced a smile on to
his face and flung open the passenger door.

"Evening, vicar!'

'Well met, Mr Cropper!' The vicar was beaming all over his face.

'Spot of business to do at school first, I'm afraid. Won't take a minute, though. Hope you won't mind waiting in the car whilst I just dash in and out.'

The vicar said he didn't mind at all, and began settling himself comfortably into his seat, just as Danny Lyndon opened the cupboard door and the body fell out.

3
Co-operation

The 'body' rolled over and sat up. It turned out to be notorious trouble-maker Connie Kellow from the top juniors—(a year ahead of Danny). Connie looked far more angry than dead.

'What—what are you doing here?' breathed Danny, considerably shaken.

'I could ask you the same thing. Proper put the wind up me you did, charging round school at this time of night.'

'I thought you were a blooming corpse.'

'I was hiding from you, if you must know. I thought you were the Cropper.'

'Did you get locked in, or what?'

'Sort of.' Connie eyed Danny warily, wondering how far she could trust him. Not far, she decided. Anybody who came to school in polished shoes and clean shirt, paid his dinner-money first thing Monday morning and never missed assembly must be on Their side. However, when Danny began explaining his own movements, beginning with the morning's Bible mishap, Connie remembered Danny Lyndon's new repu-

tation. Perhaps the lad could be trusted after all . . . up to a point. Especially if Connie could involve him in her own plans, so that he wouldn't ever be able to tell tales. Now, there was an idea!

'Like school, do you?' Connie probed. 'One of these keen types, are you?'

'It's all right.'

'You wouldn't be sorry, though, if a meteor hit it or something, would you?'

Danny shrugged. 'We'd only get sent somewhere else.'

'There's nowhere else round here to send us, now they've closed Norton Lane Primary because of the numbers going down.'

'They'd think of somewhere, don't you worry. They'd put a tent up in the park, or something.'

'Well, that'd make a nice change, at any rate. You ever been to a fire?'

'A bonfire?'

'A building on fire, stupid! A bit of real excitement, that is. Just imagine, great crackling flames and thick black smoke and everybody running about with hoses and stuff, and shouting fit to bust. Have you ever seen one close to?'

Danny's imagination made a different set of connections. Hoses—water—that leak in the Cropper's office! For a moment he'd forgotten all about it!

'Hey, you don't know where the mop is, do you?'

'Yeah, it was digging me in the ribs a minute ago.' Connie tipped her head towards the cupboard she'd just fallen out of. 'But what do you want a mop for? Going to be sick, are you?'

'There's a bit of a crisis on. Grab that bucket, will you, and come and give us a hand?'

Danny seized the mop thankfully and set off up the corridor with it, calling back a garbled explanation as he went. Connie could hardly believe her ears. 'You don't mean there's water all over the place? Oh, flipping heck, everything'll be all damp and soggy.' Connie snatched the king-size box of matches from the waistband of her jeans and hurled it into the broom-cupboard in disgust. Then she picked up the bucket and trailed sulkily after Danny.

Meantime, on a park bench a mile away from school, two furtive-looking characters were holding a guarded conversation.

'This had better be good,' said Biffer Bond. 'I was supposed to be going to see my auntie in hospital, and she's due to leave me all her money.'

'Urgent, I said it was; not good. We've nearly been rumbled.'

'Eh?' Biffer jerked back on the seat as if he had just been given a massive electric shock. 'How come?'

'I was in this pub last night, and this guy called Cropper was rabbiting on to his pal about some boring old local history society,' explained Archie Pell. 'I wasn't really listening, just sort of daydreaming over my pint, when all of a sudden I heard the name Keevan. So of course my ears pricked up and I started taking notice. It seemed there'd been an argument about the history of Keevan Tower, and this Cropper chap, who turned out to be a teacher, had gone to the library and got them to unearth a book from some back room or other, all about Keevan Tower. It's stuff they don't put out on the library shelves, 'cause there's only one copy and it's precious, being local history.'

'Blimey, they don't know *how* precious!'

'Well, this Cropper borrows the book, he says, and finds a load of stuff in it about who built the Tower and how it looked when it was first finished. You're getting my drift, are you?'

Biffer certainly was. He gave an agonised but silent nod.

'Cropper decided to take the book to school today and photocopy the bits he wanted, and although he hadn't realised it, one of those bits he was pointing out showed—wait for it!—a plan of the secret under-ground passage.'

'But you said nobody knew about that passage. You said after they'd blocked one end up, two hundred years ago, nobody ever went near it again . . . .'

'I know what I said. I was wrong, then, wasn't I?'

'Well, what are we going to *do*?'

'Just let me finish my tale before you go completely bonkers. I followed this Cropper home, didn't I, and hid myself in his privet till the lights went out. Then I tried to break in, but no joy. That house is a lot better guarded than a lion's dinner. Everything locked and bolted, even the bathroom windows. All double-glazed as well, so it was no use hurling bricks. In the end I decided to wait until today and catch him at school.'

'That was a bit of a risk, Archie. Suppose he hadn't of . . . ?'

'Well, he did. And me, I just strolled into school as bold as a bailiff and asked my way to the headmaster's office. (That's who this Cropper had turned out to be, see?) I knew he wasn't there, because I'd just seen him talking to the caretaker in the yard. Sure enough, there on his desk was this book, on top of the pile of copies he'd just made. In and out in two seconds, I was, and here they are in this suitcase, safe and sound. Now we'll have a nice little bonfire, and all will be well again.'

Biffer sagged with relief. 'Great work, Archie. You did a good job there! But let's have a look at that book before you set fire to it. Sounds interesting.'

'I only hope there's no more copies of it left.' Archie handed over a fast-disintegrating volume with the back

completely loose, and Biffer began riffling the pages. 'Yeah—that passage is marked, like you said! That was a narrow squeak, and no mistake!'

'That was the very bit he was copying, as well. He's marked the page. See here . . . ?' Archie's voice suddenly faded as he held out the top sheet of the pile on his lap. He had been stricken dumb with horror. For the drawing on the sheet was not Keevan Tower at all, but some simple geometry problem with a triangle ABC inside a circle O, and all that nonsense.

'What's up?'

Archie groaned. 'I only picked up the wrong pile of papers, didn't I?'

'Well, of all the . . . .'

'How did I know the old fool was going to put his book down on top of the wrong pile?'

'You could have *looked*.'

'Don't you dare say a word! Or *I* shall start by asking where *you* were when I was lying in the prickly privet half the night and risking my neck in the school, and . . . .'

'All right, all right; I got the message. But I suppose it'll be me that has to go back to the school now to change them papers.'

'Too late! Look at the time! School's closed long since, and he'll have taken the papers home with him. In fact, if we don't get a move on, he'll have set off for his local history meeting as well.' One agonising thought after another fled through Archie's mind. 'We've gotta stop him, Biffer. Come doom or death, we've gotta grab them papers before he starts dishing 'em out to all and sundry.'

'You're telling me!' agreed Biffer, picturing the twenty thousand packets of cigarettes from the hi-jacked lorry that were neatly piled in that underground passage. If the local history society started poking about down there it would be doom or death all right.

'Well, what are we waiting for? Where does this Cropper geezer live?'

4
Consternation

'I can't understand it,' Mr Lyndon declared. 'What the dickens has our Danny gone back to school for on a Friday night?'

'Maybe he forgot something. He was doing an art project, all bits and pieces. Easy enough to leave one bit behind.'

'Sounds very fishy to me. Didn't it strike you that he can't get back into school at this time of day? There'll be nobody there. You're too easy-going with that lad, letting him wander off just when he feels like it.'

'Oh, go on, blame me! I didn't even know he'd gone. Anyway, he was here when you came in, so you had just as much chance to notice him sneaking off as I had.'

'If it was something genuine he'd have told us. So he must be up to some mischief or other.'

'Why have you started thinking the worst of the lad lately? You don't give him a chance. He's a good lad, our Danny is. Look how he's tidied up and put the top back on his Superglue!'

'Oh yes, he's a good lad all right! That's why we just

had a bill for a new school washbasin, and all those cryptic remarks last parents' evening about trampled trees and shattered dinner plates.'

'They weren't our Danny's fault, any of those things. He told me all about them, and I believed him. They were accidents, pure and simple. Accidents can happen to anybody!'

As she said this, Mrs Lyndon suddenly clapped a hand to her mouth. Suppose Danny had had an accident just now? Suppose he'd slipped and broken his leg, or cut his head open on that nasty wall at the end of the school playground? Or even worse, suppose some kidnapper had waylaid him halfway up School Lane,

which was always deserted on a Friday night? There were some very funny characters about these days.

'Fred, what if he's in trouble? He *has* been away a long time. I think maybe you ought to go and look for him.'

'He *is* in trouble,' Fred retorted grimly.

'No, I mean hurt.' Mrs Lyndon began twisting her hands nervously together. 'You could just have a walk up to school; it wouldn't take you long. In fact, I'll come with you.'

'No; if I have to go I'll go by myself. You stop here in case he comes back. I'll find him—but I warn you, I'll deal with him properly when I do, make no mistake about that. Worrying us out of our wits!' Mr Lyndon began putting his shoes back on and buttoning up his jacket. 'We've put a lot of hard work into bringing that lad up properly. He's not going to spoil it now. A firm hand, that's what he needs while he's going through this funny phase.'

'What funny phase?' Mrs Lyndon was nearly in tears by now. 'I don't know how you can say such things! He could be lying hurt somewhere . . . .'

'And if he makes me late for my darts match, he'll be in double trouble.'

'Fred—!' called Mrs Lyndon helplessly as her husband strode off at a cracking pace. She ran up the garden path, hoping to smooth him down before it was too late. 'Don't go off in such a fury! You'll only regret it!' But Fred was already turning the corner at the top of the road.

Esmée Bates, still swinging on next door's gate, looked on with interest. 'Hey, are you and Mr Lyndon going to get divorced?' she asked with relish.

'What a blooming mess!' Connie Kellow stared enviously at the ruin of the Cropper's office. She felt quite jealous that a soft-looking lad like Danny Lyndon could have achieved nearly as much destruction in a few careless moments as Connie herself had been planning and dreaming of for weeks.

'Well, don't just stand there! Help me mop up.'

Danny was already on his knees, soaking up water as fast with his trouser-legs as with the mop. Now that he was no longer alone, Danny's panic had subsided and in fact he was beginning to experience a fine clear-headedness he had never known he possessed. Certain facts had fallen neatly into place. Connie Kellow, as well as Danny, must have climbed in through that boarded-up window, and Connie was obviously up to no good. Danny had practically caught her red-handed at something or other. Danny was beginning to feel the stirrings of power.

'How about picking those papers up and spreading them out to dry on the window-sill?'

Connie glanced up, ready with a cheeky retort, then changed her mind and did as Danny suggested. If she helped him, he'd be all the more likely to help her later on. And you never knew, if he turned out to be not quite as soft as she'd thought they might even make a team.

It was whilst Connie was dealing with the papers that she happened to glance up through the remaining window-pane—and spotted the Cropper's car turning into the far end of School Lane!

Connie said several unprintable words, two of which Danny had never heard before, then she grabbed Danny's arm and started dragging him towards the door.

'It's him! Can't let *him* in now!' ('Rotten spoilsport,' Connie was thinking, 'turning up here before I've even had a go!')

'Who—the Cropper? We're done for, then. He's got keys, so how can we keep him out?'

'We'll have to barricade the front door.'

'What with?' demanded Danny reasonably as Connie pulled him along the corridor.

'There's that big, heavy table in the entrance hall, and that great bronze bust of the idiot who opened the school. Then there's the P.E. benches, and the stuff from the office—computers and that . . . .'

'We'll never do it in time?' Yet Danny was even

35

more anxious than Connie to keep the Cropper out. He summoned up every last bit of his energy as the two of them began heaving at the great oak table. It was lucky for them that the Cropper had to fiddle with the padlock on the gate—(which both children had, of course, climbed over)—for this took up another precious few minutes, by which time the barricade was mounted. Connie Kellow had certainly proved herself as tough as any boy.

'There are all the other doors as well,' panted Danny, but Connie reminded him that all the other doors were bolted on the inside; only the front door could be opened with keys. That was a relief of sorts, but Danny immediately began to worry that the front-door barricade would never hold.

'Yeah, 'course it'll hold against a weedy old stick like the Cropper. Don't know what we'll do if he fetches the Law, though. A couple of burly constables would soon shift it.'

Danny hadn't thought of that. He didn't fancy the idea of the Law at all. In fact, it filled him with fresh panic. How had he got into this mess? Up to now, he had been a law-abiding citizen with a grudging respect for authority. He could just imagine his dad's reaction if asked to turn up at some police station to bail out his only son.

'Can't we undo the bolts and nip out the back?'

'Not likely! The Cropper would be sure to see us if we ran off now.'

'Well, let's get back in the broom-cupboard.'

'What, both of us? You must be joking! I nearly suffocated in there on my own. Besides, he'll know we're here because of the barricade, so if he gets in he'll look everwhere till he finds us, broom-cupboard and all.'

Danny turned pale, and for a moment he thought he really was going to be sick. What a final indignity, in front of Connie Kellow!

'Tell you what, though,' Connie suddenly suggested: 'We could get up on to the roof through that trap-door in the cloakroom ceiling.'

This was not such a wild suggestion as it might have seemed, for the school roof was flat, and Connie had often sneaked up there for an illicit spot of sunbathing in the summer holidays.

'The Cropper would see us on the roof all right.'

'Not him! There's that great big ledge all round. We could easy duck down behind that and wait till he'd gone.'

It was worth a try. They could already hear the Cropper rattling at the door and cursing in a most un-headmaster-like fashion. He must already have real-ised what had happened.

The two of them charged along to the cloakroom,

where they knew that the caretaker's ladder lay neatly along the floor behind the heating pipes. It was tied to those pipes with ropes, and every child was forbidden to touch that ladder on pain of instant expulsion. In no time, Connie and Danny had the knots untied and the ladder set up, though there was one heart-stopping moment when the rising ladder demolished the cloakroom light-bulb with a sound sufficient to rouse the Pharaohs.

'I'll go first,' offered Danny, more out of fear than bravery. He didn't like heights, and had once had to turn shamefully back when halfway up a lighthouse's spiral stair. He must tackle that ladder now, at once, before he had time to think. And indeed, it turned out to be surprising what you could do when death and destruction seemed to be battering at the door. Danny shot up that ladder like the temperature of an Eskimo newly arrived at the equator.

'Watch what you're doing, you nutcase!' Connie yelled as the ladder jumped and shuddered. She threw her weight against the bottom, to hold it steady, but as Danny leapt frenziedly from the top step to the safety of the upper floor, the ladder swung outwards under his final kick, then fell away in splendid slow motion, hanging for a moment in mid-air, completely unsupported, before it fell with a crash right on top of Connie Kellow.

5
Distraction

'Yes?' frowned Mrs Cropper, answering the urgently-ringing doorbell. There were two very odd-looking men on the doorstep, and her first thought was that they had come to offer to clean the drains.

'Is Mr Cropper in? We have to see him urgent,' Archie Pell announced.

'Oh—you've just missed him, actually. He's gone off to his local history society meeting.'

Mrs Cropper was about to shut the door again, but Biffer Bond had slipped his foot into the gap. 'Now, that's a pity. We'll have to go and catch him up. Where would this meeting be?'

By now Mrs Cropper had decided that she didn't like the look of these two at all. They might be planning to mug her husband, or something even worse. So she lied with commendable presence of mind—(as indeed she did whenever an irate parent turned up on the doorstep)—'I don't know where he is tonight. They choose a different meeting-place every week.'

'I wonder why they do that?' Archie began to think this local history society might not be as innocent as it

40

seemed. He took a thoughtful step forward as he spoke, and Mrs Cropper, in turn, retreated a step away from him. Before she realised what had happened, the two men were in the hall and the front door had closed behind them.

'There's no need to be nervous,' smiled Archie like a hungry crocodile. 'All we want to do is to join the local history society.'

'Yeah, we're great joiners, we are,' Biffer agreed, enthusiastically sawing the air with his heavily be-ringed right hand.

'Tell you what, if you can find us the telephone

number of the meeting-place as well as the address, we'll just have a quick word with your husband and tell him we're coming along, seeing we've left it so late. Don't want them to start without us.'

'I've *told* you, I know nothing about the meeting-place. And now, if you'll excuse me, I have a huge pile of ironing to get through whilst my husband is out.'

'Just a minute, lady! I don't think you realise how important this meeting is to us. Could be a matter of life and *death*.' Mrs Cropper did not like the way Biffer suddenly began flexing his knuckles. Wild ideas shot through her brain like a speeded-up film.

'Oh—I'll tell you what! I've just had a brainwave! His diary! He might have written the meeting-place down in there. He's very careful and methodical, you know. He writes everything down. I'll—I'll go and fetch it.'

'I'll come and help you,' Archie offered genially, taking another few steps forward. 'Don't want you to waste too much of your ironing time.'

'It's—probably in the kitchen drawer.' Mrs Cropper had some hysterical notion of being able to grab the carving-knife for self-defence—but there was no chance of that with Archie Pell breathing down her neck. Archie followed her closely from table to dresser, and there were sounds of drawers opening and shutting smartly. Of course, the diary was not there; never had been there. (As a matter of fact, Mr Cropper did not even keep a diary, dismissing them as 'schoolboy nonsense'.) They tried the living-room next, then the sitting-room, then Mr Cropper's tiny study which was really supposed to be a breakfast-room. There, at last, Mrs Cropper managed to steal a furtive glance at the clock and was thankful to see how much time had passed since her husband left home. Much more than half an hour. Mr Cropper would be safely at his meeting by now, surrounded by stalwart comrades. Thank goodness! Mrs Cropper had played for time and won. Now she could try a fresh manoeuvre.

'Silly me!' she giggled. 'I've just remembered—the meeting's at school tonight. I can't think how I came to forget! You know where the school is, I'm sure—at the top of School Lane?'

'We know!' Archie assured her disgustedly. Biffer was already making for the door.

Trembling all over, Danny Lyndon peered dizzily down from the trap-door. Was Connie dead? She was lying very still, eyes closed and a trickle of blood starting brightly across her forehead. The fallen ladder lay diagonally across Connie's stomach like a giant crossing-out. Obviously Connie needed instant help, but since the ladder had gone, Danny was trapped up there. Fat lot of help he could be! On top of the guilt and horror, Danny almost wept with frustration. Things went on getting worse and worse. The Cropper's leaking radiator was a Bank Holiday treat, compared to this. Now, Danny was faced with an emergency to end all emergencies—a '999' job, an honest-to-goodness matter of life and death. Whatever state the Cropper's room was in, whatever trouble lay ahead, Danny would have to shout to the head for help. Danny wondered what would happen to him. A long spell in prison, maybe. Well, even that was better than dragging through life with the death of Connie Kellow on his conscience. Blooming marvellous, though! You started out trying to create and make a positive contribution, and you finished up in the middle of a life of crime!

It was no use shouting from the rafters, Danny decided; no one could possibly hear him from there. He would have to venture out on to the roof all on his own. Gingerly, he progressed across the insubstantial floor and began struggling with the bolts on the little door. Finally he got the door open and emerged on to the school's flat roof. But one step more was all he took. Immediately, the lurching sky and swaying chimneys set his stomach churning. He closed his eyes and clung to the door behind him. In his imagination he had already turned giddy and hurtled from the low parapet to the ground below, where he lay splashed like a tomato on a tax-collector's windscreen. But the memory of poor Connie surfaced slowly, and Danny pulled himself together. He opened his eyes again, lowering his gaze to something more solid. That was when he caught sight of the precarious cat-walk round the edge of the roof—nothing more than rotting wooden slats with goodness knew what hazards down between them if your foot should chance to slip. How could he ever dare to walk on those? All the same, something must be done. He took a deep breath, then removed one hand from the door behind him. Next he took one trembling step forward before closing his eyes again. At last, still metres from the edge of the roof, he managed to make some sort of unintelligible croak which he hoped the Cropper would identify as a call for help. But the croak was carried away on the wind. The Cropper, busy battering at the front door with a rapidly-bruising shoulder, did not hear. In any case, he had just decided to go back to his car and consult the vicar.

'Can't get into the school!' Mr Cropper massaged his wounded shoulder. 'Someone's barricaded the door. What the dickens do you make of that?'

'Very odd,' replied the vicar. 'Are you *sure* you can't get in?'

'How could I not be sure? I've been battering the door—and myself—for the last ten minutes. I wouldn't be surprised if I've done myself a permanent injury.'

'Perhaps the lock's jammed. It happens sometimes.'

'Rubbish! Both keys turned, the latch and the mortice, but I couldn't budge the door itself. Either the caretaker's gone mad, or some of the kids are in there, up to no good.'

'Oh, I can't imagine—!'

'Well, I can! If you knew what some of those kids get up to, vicar, you'd be trying to slip your sermons into the *Jackanory* programme. Why, only today, one of 'em flung a Bible through my window.'

'Dear, dear!' The vicar looked shocked. 'What will you do, then?'

'I shall ring the police, that's what. Your phone's probably the nearest. Do you mind . . . ?'

'Don't you think that's a little drastic, fetching the police to such young children?'

'It's a little drastic for me to be shut out of my school! Drastic, and extremely inconvenient. As it is we shall be late for our meeting—if we get there at all!'

'We could come back after the meeting.'

'And find the place vandalised from top to bottom? Fish-tanks overturned, desks upended, rude writing on all the blackboards? No, thank you! Anyway, I want my sheets of paper.'

The Cropper jumped sulkily back into his car, and slammed the door so hard that the handle fell off on the outside.

46

Halfway down School Lane, Mr Cropper met Mr Lyndon hurrying along on foot. He braked immediately and wound down his window, recognising a conscientious parent when he saw one, for Mr Lyndon never missed a parents' evening or school function, and had once stood in as emergency referee for a football match when half the staff were down with 'flu.

'Anything wrong, Mr Lyndon?' Two and two were already hurling themselves triumphantly together in Mr Cropper's mind.

'Have you got my lad there?' Mr Lyndon tried to peer into the car.

'Danny? Why, no, not at this time of night. Hasn't he been home?'

'In once, then out again. Came back to school. He was seen.'

'Ah! Well, in that case—' Mr Cropper was interrupted by Mrs Lyndon, who now came panting along behind her husband in a state of terrible agitation. Arms waving wildly, she was shouting: 'Get him down! Get him down before he kills himself!'

Sensing tragedy, the vicar leapt out of his side of the car. He and the others stared first at Mrs Lyndon, then at the spot she was pointing to. There, on the roof of the school, they saw the top half of the figure of a small boy, slowly approaching the edge.

'Danny—don't jump!' yelled Mrs Lyndon frantical-

ly. Then she broke free from the vicar's restraining arm and chased on towards the school.

6
Conflagration

Soon after Danny had gone, Mrs Bodge had discovered the missing piece of Grecian vase in a geranium-pot which had shared the fateful window-sill. She slipped the fragment into her apron pocket, thinking she might call at Danny's house with it on her way home. He'd been so keen to mend that ornament, bless him! The only snag was, Mrs Bodge didn't know where Danny lived.

'Bound to be some of our kids around, though; I'll ask one of them.'

In fact, Mrs Bodge was sent off—(accidentally or on purpose, she never found out which)—in the wrong direction by a lad called Reg Hopkinson, and it was quite a long time before she decided to give up and go home. Only then, when she was halfway back home, did she come across Esmée Bates, swinging dizzily on a gate.

'Danny Lyndon? Yeah, he lives next door, but he's not in. There's nobody in.'

'Never mind, love; you can give this to Danny for me when he comes back.' Mrs Bodge held out the bit of pottery, but Esmée made no move to take it.

'He isn't coming back. He's run away from home and he's hiding in school. His mum and dad are going to get divorced.'

Good-hearted Mrs Bodge was shocked. 'Oooh, what a terrible thing! I don't know what the world's coming to, honest I don't!' She slipped the bit of pottery back into her pocket and went off in the direction of school, tutting and shaking her head. 'No wonder he threw his Bible, the poor lamb!' Well, the least she could do was to go and see if Danny was all right. Had he had a meal? Where was he going to sleep? And what sort of a state was he in? Why, the lad could do anything if he was that upset! Mrs Bodge discovered that she had quite a soft spot for Danny Lyndon, and quickened her pace.

By the time Mrs Bodge arrived at the school gate, the drama was in full swing, Mrs Lyndon weeping wildly in the vicar's arms, Mr Lyndon halfway up a drainpipe trying to reach the school roof, and Mr Cropper speeding off in his car to summon help.

'Well, I never!' cried Mrs Bodge indignantly to the vicar. 'You, of all people, mixed up in a divorce!'

'I beg your pardon?'

'Right under his nose, too, the poor lamb! Where is he?'

'On—on the r-roof!' sobbed Mrs Lyndon. 'He's

51

going to jump!'

'I'm not surprised!' Mrs Bodge would have said a great deal more, but at that moment there was a blood-curdling yell from the direction of the school and a sickening thump as Mr Lyndon fell from the drainpipe to the playground. Mrs Bodge could not help a small smile of relief. 'Oh, him! For a minute I thought you meant *Danny* was going to jump!'

Mrs Lyndon and the vicar ran to help up Mr Lyndon, who was not badly hurt. He had grazed his hands, bumped his nose and bruised himself a bit, but there was no cause for alarm. Except that he had now

realised he would not be able to reach his son by way of the drainpipe. That meant he was helpless until Mr Cropper came back with reinforcements.

'Can't we find a ladder, or something?' cried Danny's dad distractedly, dashing off on a fruitless search.

Once Mrs Lyndon was assured her husband was still alive, she returned to the front drive, whence she could keep her son in view and call to him.

'Danny—your dad's all right; he isn't hurt! Hang on a minute, love, we're fetching help. Your dad didn't mind about that hundred pounds, nor the tree and the dinner plates. If he seems a bit cross sometimes, it's just his way. Don't jump, love! Promise Mum you won't jump!'

Danny, who had no intention of jumping, could not make out what his mother was saying. All he knew was that he had been spotted, and he presumed that meant his message about Connie had been received. His knees suddenly felt weak with relief and he sat down, which put him out of sight from the ground.

'He's gone!' screamed Mrs Lyndon, making off round the side of the school. 'He's disappeared! He's going to jump from the other side! Oh, Danny!'

Mrs Bodge, who was beginning to get the hang of things, decided that, as everybody else seemed to be in a flap, she had better take charge of the situation. These three had driven the lad almost to suicide, then lost their nerve. It was up to her, Mrs Bodge, to sort the whole thing out.

Cupping her hands, she called out in her loudest voice: 'Can you hear me, Danny? It's Mrs Bodge, what helped you find them pieces. You'll have noticed there's one missing. Well, I've got it right here in my pocket. You could finish your vase in no time, then think how pleased His Nibs'd be. You don't want to do nothing silly till you've mended that vase, now do you?'

No sign from above, just a nerve-racking silence.

'Well, don't just stand there!' Mrs Bodge nagged the vicar. 'At least you could say a prayer for the lad, or think of a good quotation from the Bible.' She herself drew nearer to the school building, ready to call again, but suddenly became aware of two figures approaching the school. Could this be help? She decided to wait and see.

Archie Pell gave Mrs Bodge a friendly wave as he and Biffer Bond strode purposefully up to her. Was she going to the local history meeting, they asked.

'What, me? You must be joking! Takes me all my time to live one day at once, never mind what's past and done.'

'Well, which room is the meeting in?' asked Biffer.

'No meeting here tonight, that I do know! Though I must say there's plenty of other things going on.'

Whilst this exchange was taking place with Biffer,

Archie had moved up to Mr Cropper's window, which he remembered from his visit earlier in the day. Peering in, he saw the papers Connie had picked up and set to dry on the window-sill. They were the very ones he was looking for—the copies of the plan of Keevan Tower with the secret underground passage clearly marked. He couldn't believe his luck! He pushed at the plywood with a heavy hand, and was even more astonished when it fell easily into the room. Archie leaned in after it.

'Now, there's someone with a bit of sense at last!' cried Mrs Bodge. 'Why didn't I think of that?' She presumed, of course, that Archie was on his way through the window to rescue Danny, and ran up to give instructions: 'Go out of that door, turn left, then left again till you come to the cloakroom. There's a trap-door on to the roof. But be careful what you say; the lad's upset. Coax him, don't bully him.' She was completely flabbergasted when Archie Pell began retreating from the broken window again with his arms full of papers.

The fire-engine came clanging all the way up School Lane, with the Cropper's car following and Esmée Bates and a whole crowd of kids running excitedly behind that. Danny heard the noise and stood up again to see if it really was a fire-engine.

'There he is!' the vicar yelled. 'Now, keep still, Danny my boy, and perhaps if we were to sing a little hymn it would help? What about "All things bright and beautiful"?' In his best Harvest Festival voice, the vicar began to sing, though the sound was completely lost among the sirens and the shouts. Mr and Mrs Lyndon reappeared with more disjointed messages, and the fire-engine swerved to a halt. Immediately a turntable ladder soared into the air, bearing a helmeted fireman up towards the school roof. There was a concerted gasp, then silence. Everybody's head turned upwards.

Yes—no—yes—Danny was safely in the fireman's arms at last! Only then did the tension in the watching crowd relax. Mrs Lyndon broke into sobs and collapsed into her husband's arms, whilst Mrs Bodge was surprised to find two big tears rolling slowly down her cheeks.

'Poor little lamb!' she sniffed to the vicar. 'And after all that, they go and make it up again!'

Wrapped in a blanket, Danny babbled hysterically about some girl lying injured with a ladder on top of her, but when firemen went back on to the roof and down through the trap-door they found no sign of an injured girl. True, there was a ladder, lying where Danny must have let it fall. There was also a quantity of broken glass and a single spot of blood, and in

addition the bolts on the back door were unfastened. But there was no trace of any child but Danny. The firemen concluded that Danny was suffering from shock.

By now, as no mangled bodies were appearing, the crowd of onlookers was beginning to feel disappointed, and in fact one or two had started to drift away, when suddenly Esmée Bates cried joyfully: 'Fire!' Surely enough, there was a thick plume of smoke gliding out through the ventilator in the broom-cupboard next to the school kitchen.

7
Retribution

'Thirty copies he made; I heard him say it, not once but three times over,' Archie Pell told Biffer Bond as they sat in Biffer's lodgings counting the sheets they had rescued from Mr Cropper's office.

'Well, there's only twenty-nine sheets here.'

'We might as well have rescued none as twenty-nine. They can find out about the secret passage just as fast from one copy as from thirty million.' Archie looked exceedingly depressed, but for once in his life Biffer came up with an original idea. 'We could always move the cigarettes,' he said.

'What?' Archie was shocked at first, but slowly a grin began to spread across his face. 'You know, Biffer, I think you've got something there! But where could we move 'em to?'

'What's wrong with here? My landlady's just gone off for a fortnight's holiday. By the time she gets back, we'll have sold the lot—or smoked 'em.' Encouraged by one brainwave, Biffer had another. 'We could hire a van from that garage down the street, and drive up to the Tower first thing in the morning. We could shift 'em all in one journey then.'

'Not till tomorrow morning?'

'Nobody's going to start looking for secret passages at this time of night. It's nearly dark already.'

'Sometimes, Biffer, you amaze me!' Archie slapped his companion heartily on the shoulder, starting off a nasty coughing fit. Biffer doubled up in agony, trying to say something between the gasping, heaving, choking spasms. At last he got it out: 'For Pete's sake— gimme a cigarette!'

'Of all the rotten luck!' sneered Esmée Bates. 'Having a fire-engine right on the spot when your school starts burning down! It never had a chance!' Indeed, the firemen had made short work of the barricade, and the fire in the broom-cupboard, which had been started, they thought, by an exploding box of matches. Mrs Bodge declared that no matches were ever kept in there, which made another mystery to add to the evening's toll.

'Never mind; all's well that ends well,' declared the vicar, but Mr Cropper, making a tour of inspection, was not so sure. Those firemen seemed to have squirted water everywhere, even inside his own room, though it was well removed from the site of the fire. Everything in Mr Cropper's room was damp, and some of his possessions seemed to have been moved about rather a lot. In fact, a few of them were missing, which puzzled him until Mrs Bodge came offering to help, and told him about the two men making off with his papers. (Geometry problems? Who on earth would want those?)

'You know, Mrs Bodge, there have been some funny goings-on at this school tonight, and I don't think we've heard the last of them yet, by any means.'

'But why would anyone want to steal your papers?'

'I don't know yet, but I shall certainly look into it.'

'There's something else you ought to look into, as well. That lad, Danny Lyndon, was ever so upset about your vase. He wanted to find all the bits, so he could glue them together again.'

Mr Cropper looked up sharply. 'Oh, dear! You're not suggesting that was what made him so upset he was going to . . . ?'

'Jump? Well, it might have had something to do with it, but he was really fretting about his mam and dad splitting up.'

'Splitting up? The Lyndons? Why, they're the very last people I would have thought of . . . .' Mr Cropper sat down suddenly. 'This is a night of surprises, and no mistake! So that's why the boy got into his silly phase these last few weeks?'

'Yes, and maybe if you'd all been a bit more understanding, this would never have happened.'

A mile away, in the hospital waiting-room, Mr and Mrs Lyndon sat drinking cups of tea while Danny underwent a check-up. As the boy was still insisting upon his unlikely tale of the dying girl—(his latest version was that she had burnt up in the fire)—there had been some talk of keeping him in overnight, for observation.

'What on earth possessed the lad?' worried Mr Lyndon. 'Rampaging about on the school roof! I can't understand it!'

'I'm sure there's a perfectly simple explanation,' insisted Mrs Lyndon, 'just as there was about the sink and all those other little accidents.'

'In my experience, the word "accident" is often just an excuse for all sorts of unsavoury goings-on.'

'Well, don't forget the boy's ill. We've got to be very gentle with him.'

Mr Lyndon grunted, tenderly massaging his damaged nose and trying to ease his bruises on the hard wooden bench. If anybody was ill, he felt, it was himself, but of course it would be Danny who got all the sympathy.

Presently a nurse appeared and said that Danny could be taken home. 'I should put him straight to bed, though, without discussing this any more. And let him take things easy tomorrow. He's a bit shaken up and confused.'

Thankfully, the Lyndons collected their child and ordered a taxi to take them home. On the way they tried hard to talk cheerfully of anything but the subject on their minds.

'Well, Danny, your mother tells me you're doing a project for art, then.'

'Am I?'

'Of course you are, dear! You've just forgotten, but never mind.'

'Dad, isn't anybody going to look for Connie Kellow? She could be bleeding to death, or anything.'

'Are you still going on about ... ?'

'Sssh!' Mrs Lyndon laid a warning finger to her lips. 'Get your key out, Dad, we're nearly home.'

Mr Lyndon felt in his pocket for his front door key. It was not there. He had rushed out in such a hurry to look for Danny that he had forgotten to pick it up. Still, he remembered having told his wife to stay at home, in which case he wouldn't have needed a key. So this was all her fault.

'Have you got *your* key?' he asked Mrs Lyndon. But his wife kept her keys in her handbag, and of course you don't give a thought to accessories when you are chasing your missing son. Her handbag was still on the kitchen dresser.

'Are we locked out?' Danny showed a spark of interest. 'I could climb in through the kitchen window. Mum never shuts it properly.'

'You've done enough climbing for one night. Leave it to your dad.' Mrs Lyndon suddenly had another thought: 'Oh, Fred! Haven't you any money for the taxi, either? We'll have to borrow from Mrs Bates then, but I do hate borrowing.' She jumped crossly from the taxi and laid a hand on the Bateses' garden gate. It promptly fell apart at the hinges, subsiding to the path with a deafening clatter. (So much for Esmée's swinging marathon!) Mrs Lyndon looked shaken and upset, but Danny said, 'Never mind, Mum! It was only an accident.'

Ten minutes later, when Mr Lyndon was halfway through the kitchen window—(and a very tight squeeze he was finding it to be)—he felt an even tighter grip on his ankle and a stern voice called: 'Now then! Let's have you out of there!'

It was the local police constable, newly drafted here from country parts, and anxious to make a good job of his new assignment.

It took red-faced Mr Lyndon quite a time to extricate himself from the window, whereupon he protested that he'd lived in that house for fourteen years.

'That's what they all say,' smirked the constable, pulling out his notebook and pencil.

'But you surely don't think I'm a burglar? There's a perfectly simple explanation. The whole thing's just a little accident.'

The constable grinned. 'In my experience,' he said, 'the word "accident" is often just an excuse for all sorts of unsavoury goings-on.'

8

Exploration

'I didn't start that fire,' said Connie Kellow, meeting Danny at his gate very early the next morning.

'I never said you did.'

'No, I know.'

'How's your head?' Connie had a plaster on her forehead where she had cut it when the ladder fell.

'Oh, it's okay. How's yours?'

'Nothing wrong with my head.'

'I heard you'd been having visions, seeing dead bodies all over the place.'

'Yeah, I need my eyes testing.' Danny began to walk away, having lost interest in Connie now that he knew she was alive and well, but Connie stopped him. 'Hang about a minute! I've got something to show you. That's why I've come round here.' She began unfolding a grubby sheet of paper which she had fished out from behind the radiator in the Cropper's office the previous night.

'See that? It's a plan of Keevan Tower.'

'So?'

'So it's got a secret underground passage. Bet you

67

never knew.'

'Bet the builders never knew, either.'

'No, honest! Have a proper look!'

Danny looked. 'Huh!' he said at last.

'Suppose we go and sniff it out? Just you and me. Be a good adventure, that would.'

'No, thanks.'

'Scared, are you?'

'Let's just say I don't want to make a fool of myself, looking for something that isn't here.'

'It *says* it's there. Can't you read?'

'Then how come you're the only one that knows about it?'

Connie's lips tightened. 'Okay then, *be* like that! I can find it by myself.' She stuffed the paper into her pocket and walked away whistling.

'Danny!' Mrs Lyndon, still in her dressing-gown, peeped anxiously round the half-open front door. 'You're up early. Are you all right, love? I was going to bring you your breakfast in bed.'

'I'm fine, Mum!' Danny didn't sound it. Had he just let a perfectly good adventure slip through his fingers?

Mrs Lyndon had been going to ask, 'Was that the girl. . .?' but stopped herself just in time. Best not to start Danny off on his fantasies again. In fact, she must try to keep him occupied all day. 'Tell you what, how about coming shopping with me after breakfast? We could buy a new jig-saw puzzle and I'll help you get it started.'

Connie Kellow, never having tried to live up to anybody's expectations except her own, had no difficulty in reaching Keevan Tower very early that Saturday morning, whilst the dew was still deep enough to soak her socks and track-shoes. It was a cool day with a threat of rain, and there was nobody else about; only a self-drive hire van parked behind the Tower. She stood for a while, studying the plan she had found, and looking at the ruin with a new eye. Then she climbed over a tumbledown bit of wall that said DANGER— KEEP OUT and began carefully searching the ground.

Half an hour later, Connie came across a small hole overgrown with creepers. There was a big flat stone nearby, which looked as if it might once have covered the hole, and the creepers could be coaxed aside to reveal a flight of worn steps leading down into the earth. It was all exactly as the notes had described. Fishing out her torch, Connie started carefully downwards and kept on—until she heard muffled voices. She stopped and listened. The voices seemed to be rising from below. Could the place be haunted? There was also an eerie dragging sound—like heavy boxes being pulled along rough ground.

Well, this was a real adventure, all right! Not only was there a proper secret passage, but there was somebody—or something—actually in it! If only that Danny Lyndon hadn't been so soft, she'd have had somebody to share the fun with. ('Have to put new life into him one of these days,' Connie promised herself.)

Bravely, Connie continued her progress. It took her a few more minutes to realise that the voices and dragging sounds were getting nearer. By the time she actually caught sight of the two men, it was far too late to run away.

Danny Lyndon mooched around his back garden, kicking at bits of stone. He was utterly fed up. Since Connie's departure he had had to endure a series of excruciating scenes. First there was his dad, still smarting from his tangle with the Law, trying hard to 'understand', yet obviously resentful at the unfairness of it all, since nobody had understood *him*. Then there was his mother, treating Danny with exaggerated fuss and false jollity, as if he were royalty about to be wrongly beheaded. Worst of all, the Cropper had turned up whilst breakfast was still on the table, and had actually tried to apologise for misunderstanding everything. He had kept on casting meaningful glances, not only at Danny but at his parents too, provoking puzzlement in Mum and further irritation

in Dad. All sorts of cryptic remarks fell from the Cropper's lips, yet none of them made sense. It was worse than anything Danny had ever lived through, with the possible exception of the thought that he might have killed Connie Kellow. So what with one thing and another, the whole situation at home just now was unbearable. If this was the result of trying to live up to people's expectations, then the sooner Danny stopped, the better. He would abandon all attempts to please the grown-ups and concentrate on his contemporaries instead. Connie Kellow was the only person today who had treated Danny normally. Perhaps if Danny were to follow Connie up to Keevan Tower after all . . . ?

Danny glanced around. His mother was furtively watching him through a looped-up corner of kitchen curtain. She beamed a great, false smile when she saw she was spotted. Danny gave her a half-hearted wave, then ambled carelessly round to the front of the house—where he caught sight of Mrs Bodge, approaching along the street with a huge bunch of flowers!

That did it! Danny broke into the fastest run of his life. It took him no more than fourteen minutes all the way to Keevan Tower.

He was just in time to see two unsavoury-looking men bundling a struggling, protesting Connie Kellow

into a van and driving away. Danny noted the number of the van and ran straight home again.

'Connie Kellow's just been kidnapped!'

'Danny, where have you *been*? I thought we told you not to leave the garden today, except with one of us? You're supposed to be convalescing. And Mrs Bodge has come to see you. Look at the lovely flowers!'

Danny spun round and ran off again to find a policeman.

9
Conclusion

On Monday morning, the crowd in the school playground pressed close around its heroine, Connie Kellow. To have been kidnapped by cigarette thieves, then rescued as the thieves were caught, was enough to ensure Connie's glory for the rest of the term. But strangely enough she had turned the focus of attention on to Danny Lyndon.

'As for him, he was scared going up the ladder, and he was scared to look for that underground passage. Left me to catch them cigarette thieves on my own,' she declared, gesturing rudely at Danny who hovered on the edge of the throng.

'Fat lot of good it would have done you if they'd shredded you up for extra tobacco,' Danny pointed out. 'I was the one who set the police after you. If it hadn't been for me . . . .'

'If it hadn't been for you, capering about on the school roof last Friday, the school might have burnt down,' cried Esmée Bates.

'Yeah, trust him to spoil all the fun!'

Danny Lyndon stared at the crowd of faces, turning

now towards him and beginning to look decidedly hostile. 'There's no pleasing some folks!' he said disgustedly. He felt aggrieved that Connie Kellow should be the heroine of the moment, whilst he had had to make do with a series of tickings-off for disobeying various instructions, and being rude to Mrs Bodge. At one point on Saturday, Danny had almost begun to feel that he and Connie had shared an adventure after all; might even share others in the future. But Connie's present betrayal had hurt him badly. She ought to have been grateful for being rescued, but instead of that she'd done her best to belittle his efforts and put him in the wrong.

'You should have seen him at the top of that ladder!' Connie was jeering now. 'I don't know which of them was dithering the most. It could've killed me, that ladder could!'

'Serves you right for breaking into school in the first place!'

'I only went to get my cardigan. Anyway, hark at him! Little Goody Two-Shoes! You know what *he* was up to? He was snooping round the Cropper's desk, looking through all his papers. No wonder he always does so well in the exams!'

'You rotten liar!' Danny Lyndon saw red. He swung his lunch-bag up and lunged at Connie with it. Four salami sandwiches, one banana, one orange and a bag

of Chipples would have made quite an impact on
Connie's cheeky face. But unfortunately the lunch-bag
flew out of his hand and soared across the playground
in a wide, impressive arc. Danny closed his eyes. He
knew what was going to happen, and it did. There was
an ominous tinkling sound, followed by a more sub-
stantial crash.

'That's more like it!' Connie Kellow crowed. 'I knew
he had it in him!' She set the whole crowd cheering,
and led them in a circular war-dance round Danny.
Finally, she leapt to Danny's side, winked, held out her
hand and grinned. 'Shake!'

All at once, Danny Lyndon realised with amazement that he had achieved his life's ambition. He was popular at last.